TIZZ
ON A PACK TRIP

By Elisa Bialk

Illustrations by Susanne Suba

CHILDRENS PRESS, CHICAGO

For Gayle Harvey

This Edition Printed 1964
Library of Congress Catalog Card Number: 61-10099
Copyright, 1961, Elisa Bialk
Printed in the U.S.A.

CONTENTS

CHANCE OF A LIFETIME

Don and Tracy Hill would never forget the Fourth of July they spent at Colorado Springs the summer they were visiting their aunt and uncle's ranch. Two things happened. One was lots of fun for both, and the other turned out to be very important, especially to Don.

The fun came about when they took part in a jamboree that was held on a big ranch close to their Uncle George's Flying V. The jamboree, they had been told, was like a rodeo with local talent instead of the big-time circuit riders. Anyone could be in it, even "tenderfeet" like Don and Tracy, who had come out west only a few weeks before.

Tracy, who was eight, rode Tizz, their Palomino pony, in an event for small children. She won a silver dollar. Don, who was ten, won a silver dollar too, for being able to rope a small calf. Tracy was proud of him. He had not had much time to learn roping, but he had practiced hard at it.

Their Uncle George did not compete in anything.

Instead, he enjoyed himself talking with his friends and neighbors. Ranch people always like a good excuse to get together.

It was their Aunt Kate who won the glory for the family. Don and Tracy knew she was a good rider, but when they saw her in the ring showing her chestnut, Lucky, they realized how very good she was. To no one's surprise, Aunt Kate took first place, though she modestly claimed that it was because Lucky was such a fine horse. She did not mention the important fact that she had trained Lucky herself.

The greatest excitement came when the cowboys showed their skill at roping and bronco-busting. Don and Tracy were especially eager to see their friend, Plain Ed, ride. He was a college boy who was their uncle's summer helper, and they liked him so much that they tagged after him everywhere. That name "Plain Ed" had nothing to do with his looks—Tracy thought he was cute. It had been hung on him as a joke when he had said that he was not named Edward or Edwin but just plain Ed, and it had stuck.

The nickname, in fact, had stuck much better to Plain Ed than he stuck to the saddle of the bucking horse he came out riding as Don and Tracy, sitting on the corral fence, cheered him on. He stayed on that wildly threshing horse only a few seconds, but as it turned out, those few seconds on the bronco led to an important turn of events. Another young man in the crowd, who was as dark-haired as Plain Ed was blond, suddenly came to life.

When Plain Ed joined Don and Tracy, the dark-haired young man hurried over calling out: "Well, of all the surprises! Ed, what are you doing in Colorado?"

"Jerry Walters! What am *I* doing here? I thought you were back home in Iowa!"

"My job came through on the last day of school, and I didn't have a chance to tell you. I'm a counselor at a boys' camp just outside the Springs."

Plain Ed grinned. "Small world! I'm on the Flying V ranch, working for Don and Tracy's uncle, here. Let's get together soon."

Jerry answered, "That'll have to wait. I'm about to push off with some of the boys on a pack trip to Glacier Park."

"Boy!" Don said.

Plain Ed laughed. "I packed through Glacier with a bunch of Boy Scouts a couple of years ago, and I never had so much fun in my life."

Jerry picked him up on that quickly. "Why not come along this trip, then? We're short-handed. One of the fellows who was supposed to come out disappointed Mr. Brady, the camp director, and we're trying to get a replacement."

"Wish I could, but I couldn't let George Hill down. This is the second summer I've been with him, and he treats me like a son. But say," Plain Ed went on as the thought struck him, "how come you're taking them all the way to Glacier? You could go on a pack right here."

"These are older boys who have been out here camping before," Jerry explained. "Giving them a chance to see Glacier was part of the deal we had with them."

The two college friends talked a bit more, and then Jerry had to rejoin a group of his boys from camp. That seemed to be that, but a little while later Don saw Jerry talking to an older man he guessed to be Mr. Brady, and looking in Plain Ed's direction.

Then Don saw the older man approach Uncle George. His curiosity got the better of him, and he went over to where his uncle was sitting. He didn't exactly try to listen in, he just couldn't help over-hearing.

At first they were talking only about horses. "Why don't you rent them at Glacier?" Uncle George was asking.

"They'd cost too much for a three-week pack, and besides, they don't like to rent them out for more than a few days at a time," Mr. Brady explained. If you could let me hire two from you, I've got a trailer at the camp. It wouldn't cost anything to haul them up to Glacier."

Uncle George thought it over. "I've got only one horse I could spare right now, Shorty."

"What about that pony I've seen?"

"She belongs to my neice and nephew who are visiting me for the summer."

Mr. Brady cleared his throat. "That brings up another point. You've got a young fellow working for you who's in college with one of my counselors. Any chance of letting him go along? From what Jerry tells me, he's exactly the kind I'm looking for."

Uncle George yelped in mock pain. "First you want my horses, then you want my summer help!" More seriously, he added, "Ed's a fine boy and I hate to say no, but I need him myself, particularly this summer with my niece and nephew here. They follow him like a shadow."

Mr. Brady went on as if he were talking things over with himself: "The pack trip's for boys, so that lets the girl out. But if Ed could go, why couldn't he take your nephew along, as his helper? Then maybe the boy could take the pony," he added.

Uncle George laughed. "Glenn Brady, you certainly work all the angles! But it would be a grand experience for Don," he admitted.

"It would be the chance of a lifetime," Mr. Brady pointed out.

Don could not remain quiet any longer. "It sure would!" he shouted.

Uncle George looked startled when he realized that Don had heard every word. Then he said thoughtfully, "Maybe we could work something out. Let's talk it over with Ed—and I'll have to call my brother and see what he thinks—"

"Why don't you call Dad now?" Don suggested eagerly. "We wrote that we'd telephone home on the Fourth of July."

Uncle George stood up. He was a big man, and there

was a lot of him when he was standing. "Between the two of you, you've got me boxed in," he complained, but his voice was good-natured. "Okay, I'll see what I can do."

Don's parents were surprised, but after talking it over, they agreed that it would be a wonderful chance. They had met Ed when they had brought the children and Tizz out to the ranch, and had liked him very much. Don would be in good hands. But they wondered if Tracy would be willing to stay on the ranch without her brother and her pony. Uncle George promised to talk to her about it and not to make any plans if Tracy were not agreeable.

When Plain Ed was sounded out, he said that sure, he would love to go, as long as it was all right with Uncle George. Don was getting more excited by the minute, but he knew that there was still one big problem. What would Tracy do? He knew that Tizz meant a great deal to her, so much that she had not wanted to come out to the ranch for the summer unless the pony could come, too.

They all talked it over while they were having a chuck-wagon dinner. At first Tracy was very quiet, and Don knew that she was thinking how lonesome she might be, with her brother and her pony both gone.

Aunt Kate helped Tracy make up her mind. "You know, Tracy," she smiled, "we could have a riding school while Don is gone. I could teach you equitation on Frosty, the horse Don has been riding. Then you could teach Tizz at home next winter."

Tracy thought it over. She admired her aunt very much, and had wished often that she could ride as well as her Aunt Kate. Why, if Tizz were trained, they could ride together in the big horse show that was held every year, back home!

Tracy thought of something else, too. Don always let her ride Tizz as much as she wanted. The pony was with her much more than she was with Don. If the tables were turned and it was she who would have a chance to go on a pack trip if she could take the pony along, Don would be quick to say, "Sure, take her."

Tracy tried the words on for size, first to herself. Then she said them out loud, and they came out sounding bright and brave:

"Yes, take Tizz."

Don gave his little sister a hug. Then he ran off to

tell Plain Ed and Jerry that he'd be able to go along on the pack trip through Glacier Park.

NEW FRIEND

Don could hardly wait to get going. He talked about nothing but the pack trip, and would have trailed Plain Ed every minute of the day and night if his uncle had not seen to it that he had other things to keep him busy.

The day Mr. Brady drove up in a pick-up truck and horse trailer, Don knew that the start of the trip was at hand. The truck was packed with supplies. Uncle George drove Mr. Brady back to the boys' camp, and Plain Ed and Don loaded their own things into the truck, and Tizz and Shorty into the trailer, and were ready to set out.

"Have you got your camera, Don?" Tracy asked, and he said, "Sure." He never went anywhere without it. Last winter, he had made extra money taking pictures of neighborhood children on Tizz, and felt that he knew quite a bit about picture-taking.

When they were about to start off, Tracy almost had a change of heart, because it was hard to see Tizz going away without her. Still, she was a good sport and kept on waving and smiling after she said good-by, until the truck and trailer turned with a bend in the road and disappeared from sight.

Aunt Kate suggested brightly, "Let's saddle Lucky and Frosty and have our first lesson in school riding."

Tracy nodded, and followed her aunt to the corrals. Soon, rather to her surprise, she found that the time was passing quickly.

Don on the other hand was so excited that he hardly looked back as they left the Flying V Ranch. He was eager to see what was up ahead.

They planned to stop at the boys' camp for a briefing, and to meet the boys who would go to Glacier for the pack trip. Thinking of the new friends they would make, Don said, "I noticed Jerry Walters called you Ed and not Plain Ed."

Plain Ed smiled in his easy-going way. "Nobody at school calls me anything but Ed. The 'Plain Ed' got hung on me at the Flying V."

"Then if I didn't call you Plain Ed on this trip, nobody else would," Don figured. "I guess I'll drop it."

"It's a deal," Now-Just-Ed said quickly.

"Okay, Ed, it's a deal," Don agreed.

As they pulled into the camp, Don saw that his

Uncle George, having driven Mr. Brady back, was waiting to say good-by. He noticed, too, that some boys were also waiting, and he guessed that this would be the group to go on the pack trip. It surprised him to see that they were all bigger and older than he was, about thirteen or fourteen. Somehow, he had pictured that they would be close to his own age.

Uncle George gave Don a little notebook. "I wrote the ranch telephone number in this," he said. "Call me if you need me. And don't lose it."

"I won't," Don promised.

Uncle George made his farewell and headed back to his duties at the Flying V. Mr. Brady asked Ed to come into his office to get his schedule and route sheets. Don was left with the boys he had just met. They were friendly, but curious.

"I wish I could ride with Ed in the truck!" one of them said, and added in disgust, "*We've* got to go to Glacier Park by *train!*"

"Would you rather walk?" another boy asked, and a general snicker followed the question.

Don looked at the boy who had asked it. He was big and bright-looking, at least thirteen. A couple of the others stood close to him, shadowing him the way

Don shadowed Ed. One of the "shadows" said, "Hey, Harley, there's a pony in the trailer!"

Harley replied, "Maybe the pony will be our mascot." He turned to Don, asked him, "Or are *you* our mascot?"

"I'm Ed's helper," Don answered with quick pride.

Harley looked him over. He had to look down at him from quite a difference. Then he said, "Mascot yes, helper no." He said it in the joking way he had, but the boys around him laughed, and Don felt uncomfortable.

He was glad when Ed came out of Mr. Brady's office and they were on their way. They had a long ride ahead of them, but Ed said they would take it by easy stages. "And how'd you like to camp out at night?" he asked.

"That would be great!"

"Good. Let's do it, then. We're really going to rough it at Glacier, so we might as well start now."

That night, they made camp in a lonely part of Wyoming. Don exercised and fed Tizz and Shorty while Ed built a fire and cooked some supper. Before joining Ed to eat, Don made certain that both Tizz and Shorty were well-tethered on long lead ropes, so

they could have some freedom to graze without getting too far away. Tizz had been known to slip out of a halter rope and run away, and Don had no intention of chasing her all over what seemed like an endless prairie.

Sitting around the campfire was fun. Don felt like an early trapper or hunter. It was easy to imagine that Indians had camped at this very spot many years ago.

"Say, Ed," he started to ask, "do you suppose the Indians who lived here were Crows or Blackfeet—"

He stopped, before Ed could stop him. Both had heard a noise in a clump of sagebrush near by. It sounded like the stealthy approach of an animal.

The sound came closer. Ed, without moving his eyes from the clump of sagebrush, quietly reached for a rock. Don felt his spine chill and stiffen, but he sat where he was, quietly watching.

Suddenly, an animal came out into the open. It was a dog! He came forward on his belly, whimpering, crawling towards the fire and the food, wanting to make friends but at the same time scared.

Ed laughed and put the rock down. "I'm glad it's just a stray dog. That rock wouldn't have been much good against anything bigger!"

The dog reached Don first. He looked at him with big questioning eyes, then licked his shoe.

Don put his hand on the dog's head, and petted it. The half-forgotten gesture brought back to the animal happy memories. The sad tail went up like a waving flag. He stood up on all fours instead of crawling. Then, sensing that he was with friends as he felt Don's kindly hand, he began to bark in joyous excitement.

"Now, how in the world did that dog get 'way out here on the prairie?" Ed was wondering out loud.

"He's hungry," Don guessed by the way the dog had begun to sniff at the remains of the food.

"He's starved," Ed corrected. He opened a can of hash and watched the dog swallow the contents in a few gulps.

"Whose dog is it?" Don wanted to know.

"There's nobody to belong to, around here. Some-body must have abandoned him."

"Abandoned him?" Don repeated unbelievingly. "You think somebody would *mean* to lose him, in a lonesome place like this?"

"Well," Ed said quietly, "maybe he got lost acci-dentally from somebody who was camping around here. But you can see he hasn't belonged to anyone

for quite a while, because he's so thin and hungry." He was reaching for another can of food as he spoke.

Don looked the dog over as he was putting away another course in quick gulps. He was no special breed, just all dog. There was a lot of terrier in him, though. His hair was short, and white with black spots. He had a nicely shaped head, and his eyes were soft and appealing.

The dog used those eyes now, to look at Don as if to say thank you for the food he was getting. Don's heart turned to jelly. "Ed," he said, "we can't leave him here!"

"Who's going to?" Ed answered in his easy-going way. "He's just got himself a job with our outfit."

Don put out his hand and patted the dog again. A name came to him, right off the top of his head.

"Hello, Spot," he said.

Spot wagged his tail and licked Don's hand. He looked up as if to say, "How did you know my name?"

That night when Don curled up in his sleeping bag, Spot lay at his side. And that was where he was to stay most of the time during the whole trip, at Don's side.

LEWIS AND CLARK SLEPT HERE

The next morning, Spot awakened Don by licking his face. Then he ran to Ed and woke him up, too.

"Guess he's still showing us how glad he is that he found us," Don muttered sleepily.

"I could stand a little less gratitude," Ed confessed as he climbed out of his sleeping bag. "Besides, I think he knows it's time for breakfast, and he's still hungry."

While Ed was getting the fire going and the bacon sizzling, Don took care of Tizz and Shorty. Spot trotted at his heels. He drew back a bit when he first saw the horse and pony. Then he came up cautiously and waited to be introduced.

Shorty paid no attention to Spot. He was having a few troubles of his own, flies that had decided to come along for a free ride.

Tizz, though, was a curious pony. She sniffed at Spot, and snorted a little. Startled by the snort, Spot in turn growled deep in his throat, trying to sound tough. Then he turned tail and ran back to Ed and to that appetizing fragrance of bacon cooking over the fire.

After breakfast, Ed told Don he could exercise Tizz a little before putting her back in the trailer while he broke camp and packed up. Don rode her bareback across the prairie at a trot. At once, Spot ran after them, barking at the pony's heels.

Don was afraid the dog would frighten Tizz. "Go home, Spot!" he commanded, speaking firmly, as he had heard his Uncle George speak to his horses.

Spot, knowing he had been scolded, put his tail between his legs and scurried back to the campsite. Then a strange thing happened. Tizz stopped short, as if she were a stubborn mule, and refused to continue trotting. Don knew that if Tracy were here, she would insist that Tizz was "saying" she wanted to go back to the campsite, too.

He decided to try an experiment. "Here, Spot!" he called.

The little dog came bounding back eagerly, tail wagging. He jumped against Don, as glad to see him as if he had been away for hours. Then he was off again, barking at Tizz's heels.

But Don realized this time that the barking did not

bother Tizz at all. She started trotting briskly, swishing her pretty tail, peppy as could be, indicating plainly that she *liked* having the dog about. Perhaps his barking made up for some of the noise and excitement she had gotten used to at the ranch.

In any case, already Tizz and Spot were friends. It was with reluctance that they separated later, Tizz to ride with Shorty in the trailer, Spot to ride in the truck with Don and Ed.

Today, their route took them from Wyoming into Montana. "Boy, there must have been some exciting buffalo chases here!" Don exclaimed. "Indian wars, too, I'll bet."

"They had fun, too, though," Ed reminded. "A lot of tribes would band together for their summer encampments around here. They'd set up their tepees in rows like streets, and there'd be hundreds and hundreds of them. They'd have tribal dances, and races and sports—"

"Sounds like the Fourth of July jamboree," Don put in.

Ed laughed. "That's just about what it was, except that theirs lasted all summer."

The ride was interesting all the way. There were

always snow-capped mountains in the background, and sometimes the road dipped between flat-topped buttes with steep cliff-sides.

"The Indians used to stampede the buffalo herds and ride them over buttes like that," Ed said as he pointed one out. "That was easier than hunting them down one by one—sort of an early-day production line."

Don nodded excitedly. "I learned about that when we had Indian Month in Cub Scouts. We made coup sticks for our Pack meeting."

"That's a good way to learn," Ed agreed. "Now, watch for historical markers. We're getting into Lewis and Clark country — they crossed the Continental Divide not far to the west from here."

"Do I wish I could have gone along with *them!*" Don blurted with such emphasis that Spot jumped. "That was real pioneering."

Ed grinned. "For a city boy of ten, you're doing pretty well at roughing it, yourself."

That night they camped out again, near the city of Missoula. Ed said Missoula was famous for its university, but Don was more impressed by a marker he read which told him that Captain Lewis had camped at Rattlesnake Creek and Clark Fork, and then had passed through Hell Gate Canyon.

Spot had ridden in the truck with his nose out of the window, sniffing the air as excitedly as if he too were imagining the Indian battles, the buffalo hunts, the summer encampments, and Lewis and Clark making their brave but slow trek to the Pacific. When Ed parked the truck for the night, though, he jumped out and ran back to the trailer and waited with eagerly wagging tail for Tizz to come down the ramp and to be tethered on a long lead near a stream. Then he stayed close to her, frisking about until it was time to eat.

The next morning no one was in a hurry to start on the last lap of the trip, Tizz and Spot least of all. Tizz had to be coaxed back into the trailer with some of the carrots Tracy had packed for her, and Spot looked forlorn as the door closed between him and his pony friend.

Today's drive was a short one, through a few western towns and a lot of beautiful country. They could easily have reached Glacier Park by nightfall, but they were in no hurry, as the boys and Jerry were not due to arrive until the next morning.

At Don's suggestion, Ed agreed to camp that night outside of Belton, and the park entrance. Alone with Ed, Don found it easy to imagine that he too was grown up, and keep on pretending that he was an early trapper or hunter. He remembered how big those boys were who would come out for the pack trip, and how small he felt next to them.

When they were ready for sleep that night, Don looked up at the stars and wondered how many Flatheads and Blackfeet those stars had watched. And Lewis and Clark, and all their brave men. . . .

"Say, Ed," he called, and Spot, curled close to him, started out of his sleep at the unexpected sound of his voice, "were Lewis and Clark up around Glacier, too?"

"Lewis was," Ed answered sleepily. "You heard about what happened on the way back from the Pacific—he and Clark separated, and he came this way with a party to explore the Marias River."

"I remember reading about it now!" Don cut in. "That's when they were attacked by Indians."

"Well," Ed corrected, "I guess *attacked* wouldn't be the word. The Lewis party caught the Blackfeet in their camp, and there was kind of a free for all, and when it was over a couple of the Indians were killed. So Lewis and his men left in a hurry and made it back to Clark and the rest of the expedition."

"Boy!"

Don thought about that exciting encounter, and was about to ask another question when he realized that Ed was asleep. So was Spot. The little dog was twitching in his sleep, as if he were fighting Blackfeet himself.

Presently Don fell asleep, too, still thinking about Indians. He awakened to the sound of Spot's low and ominous growling.

Opening his eyes, Don looked directly into the face of a tall Indian wearing war paint and a full headdress.

Don was more than startled, he was scared. But he pulled himself together and decided he would have to pretend to be brave. He wanted to speak, so that he might wake up Ed.

Managing to keep his teeth from rattling, Don said, "Me, Don Hill. Who you?"

The Indian looked at him for a moment, without a change of expression. Then he answered, not only in perfect English but with an eastern school accent: "Why, I'm Freddy Steppingstone. Sorry if I fright-

ened you, but I'm taking my usual shortcut to the park. Forgive me for seeming immodest, but they tell me that I'm quite a tourist attraction."

A chuckle came from Ed's sleeping bag, followed by Ed's voice: "Hi, Freddy! You still around?"

Freddy Steppingstone folded his arms solemnly across his chest and said, "How!" Then he smiled broadly, in an un-Indian fashion, as he added in the voice that sounded so funny coming out of that Big Brave get-up: "Naturally! Why, the park could hardly get along without me. And since you're now awake and about to have breakfast, no doubt, I'll be glad to accept your invitation to join you. Perhaps I may even ride the rest of the way in your truck, beneath my dignity though it may be."

"Be careful," Ed warned with a laugh, "you're speaking of the truck that I love."

They joked all through breakfast and during the ride into the park. Don was so fascinated that he kept staring at Freddy Steppingstone almost as much as he gaped at the enormously high peaks and glaciers that presented such imposing views up ahead.

"I shall see you again," Freddy Steppingstone promised as they dropped him off at the park headquarters.

"I am like the bad penny that keeps turning up everywhere."

Don and Ed said good-by and Spot wagged a farewell. Then they headed for the station to meet the morning train, and the boys with whom they were going to live for the next three weeks.

BEARS!

Jerry Walters stepped off the train first, and the boys jumped off eagerly after him, each carrying a small pack.

Jerry was glad to see Ed. He grinned with relief as he said, "I began to wonder what would happen, if you got stalled somewhere along the way with the supplies."

"Why, my helper and I wouldn't let you down," Ed assured him, and Don hoped the boys heard him.

As the boys gathered in a group, Don, still feeling important, blurted out, "Guess what we've got? A dog!"

If he had meant to get their attention, he had it. "You have?"

"Where is it?"

"How did you get it?"

The questions came thick and fast. Don led the boys over to the pick-up truck and showed them Spot in the front seat. The little dog, happy to see Don, wagged his tail and barked a greeting.

Don told the boys how Spot had come to them out of the sagebrush the first night they camped in Wyoming. "He was half-starved," he added, "but I think we're starting to fill him up, finally."

"He looks like a good dog," the boy he remembered as Harley decided. "Now we've got two mascots, the pony and the dog."

Don was not sure he liked that "we," but he let it ride. Ed and Jerry, after a brief confab, were ready to start moving.

Don rode ahead with Ed in the truck, while the boys hiked to Avalanche Creek Campsite with Jerry. As they swung into the park along the main highway, an awed sigh escaped from Don, like air let out of a tire. He had never seen anything so beautiful as the scenery up ahead.

They passed a lovely sparkling blue lake to the left. "That's Lake MacDonald," Ed told him, and added with a chuckle, "I'll never forget what happened the last time I was here. Some of us were out in a boat when a moose came swimming along. Its antlers were six-feet across. We sure got out of its way in a hurry."

"Do moose attack people?" Don asked in surprise.

"Not when they're swimming, but sometimes they charge them. If you see a moose, it's better not to wait around and see what it's going to do."

At the campsite, Ed told Don they were going to unload everything they would need for the pack trip, then leave the truck until it was time to go home. "We can't take it with us on the high trails where we're going," he explained. "That's why we've got to use pack horses."

That reminded Don that Tizz had not yet had her morning carrot. He fed it to her through the door of the trailer. She munched it slowly, for Tizz, looking at Don wistfully in the meantime. He could see she was asking him to please let her out, and perhaps take her for a little run. But she would have to wait a little longer. There was work to be done.

Don was still helping Ed with the job of setting up camp when he could hear the boys coming. They sounded excited, and when they got there, it was easy to see that they *were* excited.

"Guess what?" Harley shouted before anyone else could. "We saw a bear and her cub, right back there along the highway!"

"You did?" Don commented, trying to sound properly impressed. He was not sure that he would like to meet a bear and her cub while he was walking.

"Yes. The bear was begging for food. If you hurry, you can still see them," Harley suggested.

Don turned to Ed. "Are they wild?"

"Well, they're not tame. That's why you're not supposed to touch them or tease them."

Harley said, "Roy here got some pictures close up. I see you brought your camera. Why don't you go back and get a picture, too?"

Don asked Ed, "Could we drive over?"

"Not right now, Don. Jerry and I have some things to do first."

"Then I'd better stay and help you," Don decided quickly, and there was relief in his voice.

The tone of relief was not lost upon Harley. "Sure," he smiled, "you better stay here and help. Ed and Jerry need you."

Don did not like the way he smiled.

When the work was done, Jerry called the boys together. "Okay, fellows," he announced. "We're going to hit the trail for Avalanche Lake. It's the easiest hike in the park, but it will be a good way to unkink. Follow me, and stay together."

They set out. Don looked after them uncertainly. "Do we get to go along?" he asked Ed.

"Tizz and Shorty need exercise," Ed answered thoughtfully. "Tomorrow, they start being pack ponies. Want to ride instead of walk while you've got a chance?"

"Sure," Don said promptly. He knew Tizz was pretty anxious for a fast trot. She told him so, too, by neighing impatiently as he saddled her.

Ed rode on ahead because he knew the trail. Spot raced joyously alongside of Tizz, wagging his tail so fast in his excitement that Don wondered why it did not snap off.

They caught up to the hikers at a dam which beavers had built over Avalanche Creek. "Hey, I thought you said that was a *pack* pony!" Harley challenged when he saw that Don was riding.

"She'll be my pack pony here," Don explained, "but at home, I ride her."

"You mean on a ranch you ride a *pony?*" Harley said in a disbelieving voice.

Don did not want to stop to explain that his uncle's ranch was not really "home" to him, and that Tizz belonged not only to him but to his little sister. "Well, she's my pony," he said simply, thinking that would settle it.

Harley said no more about it. But he looked at Roy and Dick, the two friends who were his shadows, and he smiled in that funny way again.

Ed and Don rode on to Avalanche Lake. Because it was still early in the season, heavy cascades from Sperry Glacier in the background poured down its wall into the lake. It was a beautiful sight, but Don thought it sure looked cold.

Since they wanted to give the boys a head start, they rode around the lake a bit, exploring while Ed identified some of the near-by peaks and glaciers. "That's Mount Cannon," he said as he pointed to a huge one. "It was named after the first woman who climbed it. It used to be called Goat Mountain. There are a lot of mountain goats here, but you've got to look hard to find them."

"I'd like to get some pictures of the mountain goats," Don decided.

"Sure, so would everybody else. But that won't be easy. They stay above the timberline. You'll have to keep your eyes open."

They rode so long that the boys and Jerry got

back to the campsite ahead of them. Don could tell they were back by the noise they heard as they came down the trail.

It turned out that the bear and cub had come into the campsite while everyone was gone. The bear had scnt her cub scurrying up a tall pine, where the baby was crying for her mama like a spoiled child.

"That's an old trick of theirs," Ed explained, "—using a tree as a 'sitter.' The cub's mother is probably hunting for dinner." He scooped up Spot, who had begun to growl deep in his throat, just to play it safe.

Before gathering around the pine as the other boys had gathered, Don decided to tether Tizz first. He wasn't going to have to chase her all over Glacier Park!

The job completed, he began to walk towards the big pine for a closer look at the cub. Suddenly, Jerry shouted, "Here comes the mother bear, boys. Step back and let her through."

Don turned his head. There was the bear, coming right at him, or so it seemed.

This was the first time he was meeting a bear face to face outside of a zoo. Without thinking, Don turned and ran back where he had come from, which meant that he ran back to Tizz.

He heard a laugh, and a voice that he recognized as belonging to Harley: "That pony may be our mascot, but she's Don's bodyguard."

Roy and Dick laughed, too.

Don gritted his teeth. He knew he was going to have trouble with Harley.

GOING-TO-THE-SUN

Jerry had the boys up early the next morning and on the trail leading to the imposing Garden Wall and Going-to-the-Sun Mountain. They were heading for the Granite Park area, which would be headquarters for a couple of days, and a long hike lay ahead.

Ed and Don stayed behind to pack the supplies. This first time, Ed wanted to show Don just how to do it. First he placed a thick blanket on Tizz's back, for protection, and fastened it securely with a cinch. Then he divided a supply of tinned and packaged foods in saddle bags, and set an equal weight on each side of Tizz, for balance. He was careful to see that the pony did not carry a heavier load than she would be carrying if someone of Don's size were on her back.

Shorty, a strong and chunky horse, would carry the brunt of the load. A pack carrier that looked like a wooden sawhorse set upside down, was placed on top of the protective blanket on Shorty's back. This was then filled with supplies, and Ed was again careful to see that the load was evenly balanced on both sides. In this way, he explained, a horse like Shorty could carry up to three-hundred pounds without being overloaded.

When the packing was finished, Don was eager to set out on the trail, hoping to catch up to Jerry and the boys before long. Spot, too, was in his glory as he started out. New sights and sounds and smells kept him in a high pitch of excitement. He tried to chase everything he saw, even a porcupine, before Ed caught him and held him back. He chased a deer which swiftly outran him, and Ed cautioned, "Better not try that on a moose!"

Tizz, though, was not in equally good spirits. It was not the weight she objected to, Don was sure. She was an independent kind of a pony, and having something tied to her was not to her liking. It was going to take awhile to get used to it. In the meantime, she paused often to snort or shake her head as if she were chasing off flies. Sometimes she would stand stock still and would not move even though Don urged her on, and they would fall quite far behind Ed and Shorty. Only Spot seemed to be able to get Tizz to move, then. The little dog would come scampering back, barking questioningly as if to ask what was the delay. Then, as he ran on ahead again, Tizz would start up, also.

Looking at that great Garden Wall, Don wondred how they were going to make it at the rate they were going. Glaciers and cathedral-like peaks and spires formed a fascinating pattern that seemed to keep changing constantly. Going-to-the-Sun Highway led right up alongside of it, extending to Going-to-the-Sun Mountain.

At first the trail they were following ran along a rushing stream and was in deep shade and green forest. Then it opened into a fire-scarred area which showed sadly what could happen to beautiful country when fire swept through it. Ed told Don that the big fire had burned down hundreds of acres of trees that had stood nearly a hundred feet high and, although it had happened years ago, the new growth was barely getting started.

Up ahead lay a hard climb, with the trail ascending sharply. Right here, in a clearing at the trailside, lay the boys of the outfit and Jerry, taking a lunch break. Some were still eating the sandwiches and apples they had packed in their knapsacks early this morning.

"Where've you been?" some of the boys called when

they saw Ed and Don approaching. "Did you get lost your first day out?"

Ed smiled good-naturedly. "Tizz was a little slow this morning. She's not sure she likes being a pack pony, and she's letting us know it."

Harley spoke up. "At camp when the mules won't get going, they use a stick on 'em. Maybe that's what you'll have to do with your pony."

Don heard himself saying sharply: "You better not try it with Tizz!"

Ed said in an undertone, "Simmer down, he's only kidding," and Don calmed down. But the sandwiches that had looked so good when he had made them this morning tasted awfully dry when he tried eating them.

Whoever else might be kidding, Jerry had not been when he had said that today's hike was a tough one. It was not until late afternoon that the party reached the campsite.

Don was dog-tired. The others had made long hikes like this before, and were used to mountain-climbing. That was why they had wanted to make the pack trip to Glacier. For him, it was the first time, and he was the smallest besides. Still, he wanted to help Ed with the unpacking. Ed took one look at him, then said in his easy way, "You better loaf around awhile. I'll un-pack Tizz and Shorty, and you can give them their rub-down later."

This was fine with Don. He sat down, for once glad that he *could* sit down, and looked toward the valley from which they had come today. Because the climb had been gradual, he had not realized they had climbed so high.

As Don was resting and appreciating the view now that he could enjoy it, Roy and Dick came running towards him. "Harley just saw a moose!" Roy called.

"You've got your camera right with you," Dick suggested. "Come on back with us, and we'll show you where the moose is."

Don got to his feet slowly. He looked around for Spot, but the dog was with Ed. He remembered what Ed had said about a moose, and he was not sure that he wanted to get close enough to one to take a picture. But he also thought of the way the boys had laughed yesterday when he ran away from the bear.

That thought seemed to turn Don's feet in the direction Roy and Dick were leading him. The boys ran to the edge of a stand of trees. Sure enough, over the top of some bushes in the half-light of dusk, Don could see a wide spread of antlers.

He slackened his pace. "Ed said that a moose some-times charges at people," he recalled.

Even as he spoke, the antlers moved ominously towards him. There was a forward movement in the bushes.

Don did not stop to wait and see if a moose broke out. He just turned and ran. Only then did he hear a laugh that was becoming all too familiar to him.

When he looked around, he saw that it was Harley who had come out of the trees. He was holding two long branches over his head at a horizontal angle. He might have thought he looked like a moose, but to Don, his laugh sounded like a hyena's.

At supper, Jerry said, "The ranger will give a talk at the campsite grounds tonight, and there'll be a bonfire and sing. How many of you would like to go?"

Don watched the show of hands. No one, it seemed, was too tired to go, even after the hard day's hike. His own hand went up, too, last but not least.

Yet, tired or not, he was glad that he heard the ranger speak. He described the wild life that could be found, and rare trees and flowers to look for. He also told some Indian legends, and how Going-to-the-Sun

Mountain came to get its name.

The Indians believed that, many years ago, a wise Old Man had lived among them and had created the world and everything in it, including man and woman. He had taught them how to make bows and arrows so that they might have food, and how to use roots and herbs to cure their ills. When they had learned all he could teach them, then he said it was time for him to return to the sun. He set out along the trail to the tall mountain, and then when he reached it, he disappeared behind it in a blaze of light.

Don liked that story. On the way back to their own camp, he asked Ed if it was true.

"Sure," Ed answered, "it's as true as any story."

True or not, Don decided to believe it. It made this beautiful park seem like a magic one.

Don said good night to Tizz, as Tracy would have done, and then he curled up to sleep with Spot. He could hardly wait for the next day to come, with its further adventures. If only Harley. . . But Don did not bother to finish the thought. He was asleep.

THE HIGH TRAILS

The plan was to make the Granite Park area head-quarters for several days, taking side trips from that base. An easy excursion was planned for the first day. On the next, Jerry took the boys to Logan Pass and Hidden Lake.

The trail ran along the Garden Wall and was a narrow one, for foot traffic only. Ed stayed back at camp, to keep an eye on Tizz and Shorty, do a few needed chores, and have some hot chow ready when the boys came back hungry in the late afternoon. He urged Don to go along because he said Logan Pass was something no one should miss, and he knew what he was talking about because he had been there before.

Don decided to go along with Jerry. Then Spot had to make up his mind whether he wanted to go with Don or stay with Tizz. The little dog ran back and forth between the two, having trouble making a decision. Finally, the chance for a new adventure won out. He caught up to Don, looking back as if to apologize to his pony friend.

Don found that today's hike was not an easy one, either. Water from melting snow and ice still trickled down from the peaks and formed cold pools along the trail. On one side, there was the protection of that rocky wall of peaks, but on the other there was Going-to-the-Sun Highway, which seemed to hang on the very edge of the cliff.

The valley from which they had climbed and Avalanche Creek Campsite, which had been their first headquarters, were far, far below. It made Don dizzy to look directly down into that valley from the height of the trail along the Garden Walk, but he was careful not to let Harley see this. He had come to feel that the more he stayed out of the bigger boy's way, the better off he was.

Today's trail was hewn out of the steep cliff-side all the way to Logan Pass. There, Don was surprised to find snow. The ranger said it had been cleared off Going-to-the-Sun Highway by plows, and that the restaurant and souvenir shop at Logan Pass had been snowed under until just a week or ten days before.

Don, who had brought his camera on the hike, got some pictures of the snowbanks. Jerry suggested that he could get more interesting shots of the glacier they would see on the way to Hidden Lake.

"You might even see some mountain goats," he added. "I've never walked to Hidden Lake without seeing a few, myself."

Don felt the thrill of being an explorer as he set off following Jerry along the trail that led across a meadow. Even though there were some lingering patches of snow here, too, the warm sun that bathed the meadow was already bringing up a variety of alpine-type flowers.

As they passed a spring where water trickled into a stream, Jerry called Don's attention to a little bird flying in and out of the trickle. He said it was a water ouzel, a little mountain bird that nested right under the falls. Don tried to get a picture but the light was bad.

He brought out his camera again when they came to the glacier Jerry had told him about. He asked some of the boys to pose sliding on it. Roy and Dick did as they were asked, while Don checked his light meter, but Harley grew impatient.

"Come on," he urged. "We can't stand here all day."

"Just a second. I'm getting a reflection I don't like,"

Don said professionally.

"Big deal!" Harley muttered

Don felt self-conscious, but he took the time to get the picture the way he wanted it, anyhow. He thought it would sound like boasting if he told Harley that he had earned money with his camera last winter, so he let it ride.

Spot chased a ground squirrel, but it got away so fast that Don was not able to get a picture of it. He did manage to get one of Spot in hot pursuit, though, and he thought that might turn out to be even better as a souvenir.

But today the mountain goats were not to be found. Jerry scanned the cliff-sides, above timberline, with his binoculars, but could not see any. "They usually travel in herds," he said, "and you may see several of them suddenly, so keep your eyes open."

Don tried hard to follow Jerry's advice. Descending the steep trail that led to Hidden Lake, he suddenly spied the white patches Jerry had told him to look for, on a near-by peak.

"There they are!" he cried. "There are the goats!"

Everyone stopped to look, even Harley, who must

have wished that he had been the first to see them, himself.

Don focused his camera. In order to get a better angle, he stepped back.

Just then Spot saw a small furry animal that got his immediate attention. The little dog leaped behind Don just as he stepped back. The footing was slippery at best and, thrown off balance, Don fell over backwards. He was still pointing his camera, all right, but now he was pointing from a horizontal position and getting nothing but blue sky.

Jerry reached out a hand to help him up. "Are you hurt?" he asked.

"Heck, no," Don answered, scrambling to his feet quickly. A check of his camera equipment proved that nothing had been hurt but his pride.

Then an all-too-familiar snicker came to his ears. Harley added along with the snicker: "That kid needs his bodyguard. He shouldn't climb trails without his pony. She's more sure-footed than he is."

As usual when Harley made a comment, Roy and Dick laughed.

Don, cleaning himself off from his muddy fall, muttered to Jerry, "I could murder him!"

"Take it easy," Jerry advised. "Do what Ed does when anybody kids him."

"What does Ed do?"

"He just grins and bears it. People find it's no fun teasing people if they don't get mad."

Don tried to smile. The trouble was, he just did not feel like smiling, and he couldn't quite make the grade.

What was worse, he did not get his picture of the mountain goats, because when he tried again to focus his camera in their direction, they had moved behind an outcropping of rock.

"Don't worry," Jerry soothed, "you'll have plenty of other chances. And those were pretty far away."

"But at least I could have proved that I *saw* them," Don said.

He hated to muff a chance like this, and he hated to go back to the campsite later and tell Ed that he had muffed his chance. Even if Harley didn't think much of him, he wanted Ed to admire him.

DON GETS HIS GOAT
AND HARLEY'S, TOO

Don had not yet gotten that goat picture he was so anxious to get when the outfit packed over to the Going-to-the-Sun campsite. He was an experienced camper by now, though, and was able to pack the supplies Tizz would carry with just some final help from Ed, in lifting up the load, and tightening the cinch.

Jerry praised him by saying, "You know, Don, you do all right for a little shaver!" Don was pleased that Jerry thought he was earning his way. The pack trip's leader had not started out a friend, as Ed had. Don knew that so far as Jerry was concerned, he had to prove himself, and he was glad he seemed to be doing it.

But there was no praise coming from Harley. Instead, that boy still seemed to have an uncanny knack for being around whenever anything happened that put Don in a bad light.

Tizz was becoming an experienced pack pony by now, too. She no longer was annoyed by the weight on her back with nobody riding, as she had been the first day, and moved along as nimbly as Shorty. She and Spot were inseparable except at night, when Spot wisely chose to share Don's warm sleeping bag.

The first night at the new campsite, the boys went to hear another lecture by a park ranger. The lecture dealt with the different Indian tribes who had lived in this part of the country, and with their customs and rituals.

A pleasant surprise was in store for Don and Ed. Freddy Steppingstone turned out to be the "Indian chief" who was demonstrating some ritual dances. He seemed as solemn and majestic as Going-to-the-Sun Mountain, but when they talked to him later, he was the same old Freddy, still enjoying his little jokes, and surprising people by talking offstage with his careful diction and eastern accent.

Don wished he could get a picture of Freddy, to keep as a souvenir and to show Tracy later. But the first time he had seen Freddy, at that early-morning meeting, his camera had been packed away in the truck. Tonight, it was too dark.

Hearing Don say that he wished he could get a photo, Freddy nodded and said: "It would indeed be a misfortune not to be able to preserve these features from generation to generation." Though he spoke solemnly, his eyes twinkled. "However," he continued, "hope glimmers on the horizon. Next week, Freddy Steppingstone will be the main attraction at Two Medicine Lake. Ed here tells me that your schedule calls for you to be at Two Medicine then. I shall gladly allow myself to be coaxed into coming out in bright daylight for the photograph you long for."

"That'll be great!" Don said. His speech was much more direct than Freddy Steppingstone's, but it was full of real enthusiasm. He was glad to know that he could look forward to seeing Freddy again, too. The Indian, in or out of character, was fun.

The morning after the lecture the boys were up early, as usual, and even a little more excited than usual. They were going to climb Going-to-the-Sun Mountain. At least, some of them hoped to make the climb. Those who found the going tough would stop along the way and wait for the others.

Jerry had climbed the mountain on previous visits, so it had been decided that he should be the one to lead the boys on the climb. Ed would take his turn at keeping the campfires burning.

This time when Don offered to stay back at camp with him, Ed let him. Spot stayed, too, though he looked with longing after the departing hikers.

When the others had gone, Ed said, "Jerry and I felt you were too young to try such a hard climb, Don. It's not fair to expect you to go as fast as the bigger fellows."

Don made no comment. He could see the point, but he hated to admit, even to himself, that he might not be able to keep up with boys like Harley.

What Ed said next cheered him up a lot. "I have an idea how we could have some fun on our own today. Let's go fishing."

"Sure, let's," Don agreed quickly. Then he remembered, "But I thought we were supposed to keep an eye on Tizz and Shorty."

Ed grinned his easy, pleasant grin. "I've got that all figured out. We'll take them along. In fact, we'll ride them."

"The saddles are still locked up in the truck back at Avalanche Creek," Don reminded.

"Who needs saddles? Why can't we ride the way the Indians rode? That's the way you've been exercising Tizz, anyhow."

It sounded like fun, as it turned out to be. They mounted bareback and rode off towards a mountain stream where Ed had heard the fishing was good.

Spot went along, of course. The only trouble was that the little dog became so excited when they were on the move and he was seeing new places and smelling new scents, that he wore himself out. Actually, he covered about twice the distance that Tizz and Shorty covered, because he ran up ahead, then back, or he circled widely as he detoured to investigate some motion in the bushes. Finally, Don scooped Spot up and put him in front of him, where he lay across Tizz's neck, "talking" to his pony friend by making short yapping noises.

Being with Ed was always interesting as well as fun because Ed seemed to notice everything. He called Don's attention to some alpine larch, a tree which the ranger had told them about just yesterday, and had suggested that they look for because it was quite rare. Don got a picture of it. Personally, he would rather get those hard-to-find mountain goats, but he knew that his mother would like to see the larch when he got back home.

As they rode to the stream Ed had in mind, Don

kept looking up towards the surrounding peaks, watching for the goats as usual. "You're going to have a permanent stiff neck if you don't get that picture soon," Ed kidded, and Don replied that he wouldn't mind if he did—as long as he could see the goats, too.

At the stream, Don let Tizz and Shorty drink and graze. While Ed was casting for trout in the rushing water, he and Spot followed its course, watching for water ouzels nesting under the protection of falls.

There was a point where the stream ran close to a higher peak. Through force of habit, Don looked up at it. Then he almost gave one of Spot's excited little yelps himself, because there they were, on the mountain across from him—five mountain goats.

What was more, these were close enough so that he could see what they looked like. After all his neck-craning, here they were before his very eyes, and Don would probably never get any closer! And this time, there was no slippery trail and no leaping dog to upset his plans.

Don worked fast enough not to lose his chance, but he thought the whole thing through carefully. He considered light and distance, and he got the right composition. Then he snapped several pictures before

the goats moved out of range, and he felt pleased that he had gotten them exactly as he wanted.

When he returned upstream to where he had left Ed and Tizz and Shorty, he found that Ed was pretty

pleased himself. He had caught two trout, both "keepers," and he said they would have them for lunch.

Don found that Tizz was quite pleased, herself. She had discovered a patch of fine grass and was having quite a treat. Don waited to give her a chance to have her fill, before heading back for camp.

He was pretty eager to get back, though. Excited about having seen the goats and gotten his picture, he wanted to pass the good news on to the rest of the boys.

There was still a wait ahead of him. The day's climb had been a hard one, and it was not until twilight that Jerry and his outfit came hiking in.

What Don did not know was that Harley was pretty pleased, himself. He had been among the few who had gone right on to the top of Going-to-the-Sun Mountain, and the climb had not been easy. For him, too, it had been a first. He was as anxious to tell about the climb as Don was to tell about the goats.

So when the boys approached and Don called to them, "Guess what? I finally got my goat!" Harley answered in usual Harley fashion.

"Mine, too," he muttered, and of course, Roy and Dick added their laughs.

Don felt hurt, and Don felt mad. A sharp answer came to his tongue, but he remembered Jerry's advice about smiling the way Ed smiled when he was teased.

This time Don managed to smile. It was not easy, but he smiled.

THE AVALANCHE

It was time to move on to another campsite. The next one would be at Many Glacier.

As usual, Ed wanted to get a head start and arrive ahead of the boys and Jerry, so he could make camp and have a hot supper waiting for them.

Don started out with Ed soon after breakfast at sunrise. Seeing the sun come up and reflect its red glow in the glacial peaks, and the sparkling blue lake waters, was something Don was not likely to forget in a hurry.

Tizz was frisky with Spot trotting along at her side, or making brief excursions into the bushes and reporting back to her. As for Don, he felt that with Ed he could have a good time anywhere, and here in this beautiful rugged country, he couldn't miss.

This morning they followed the Piegan Pass Trail, which ran along a creek until it came to some falls. Then it branched off and began climbing. It underpassed Going-to-the-Sun Highway, which by now had become as familiar to Don as the Garden Wall.

Again, the trail led along a creek and through a forest which opened into a lovely meadow. Picture-postcard views opened up in every direction, with mountain peaks surrounding them, and Don became a bit "camera happy" as he tried to snap pictures in all directions.

When they came to Lunch Creek, they agreed without argument that this was the place to stop and eat. Today, Don's sandwiches, which he had made when it was not quite daylight, tasted awfully good. He wouldn't have given up this chance to come to Glacier Park for anything in the world, but to himself he had to admit that he always had the best time when Harley was not around watching him.

Starting up again when they had eaten and Tizz and Shorty were rested, Ed and Don soon came to Piegan Pass. It was at the top of an open park, and from it they could see the Garden Wall and the Going-to-the-Sun Mountain. From Piegan Pass, the trail began to descend in rocky and steep switchbacks. The going was slow and tricky.

The going became even trickier when they came to Morning Eagle Falls, where a thin sheet of water poured over red cliffs. The trail here was wet, too.

Snow was still melting from the top of the peaks, since it was early in the summer.

After they made a turn in the trail and were cutting back in another direction, they heard a heavy sliding noise behind them. "What was that?" Don asked.

Ed had stopped to listen. "An avalanche. There are a lot of small ones when it's been a late wet season —you remember the rock piles you saw along Going-to-the-Sun Highway at the Garden Wall?"

Don nodded, remembering. He was glad the avalanche was behind them.

They had hardly gone more than a dozen feet when they heard the sound again. This time, the slide was above them. Don, bringing up the rear, stopped short with his hand on Tizz's lead. The pony stood still without panicking. Spot, too, stood still, pointing his stubby tail, all attention.

But Shorty, up ahead, became frightened. He reared up on his hind legs, pack and all, and Ed stepped back to calm him.

The slide was right above Ed and Shorty. Ed knew this, but he still held his ground, calmly trying to save his horse and pack. He brought Shorty down with a

firm hand on his lead rope, and pushed him backwards.

The first small rocks of the slide were tumbling
down on them as Ed pushed Shorty out of the way.
He would have made it himself without any trouble,
if Shorty had not panicked again. He lunged forward,
then jerked back, and in that unexpected forward
movement, he knocked Ed off balance.

Ed fell down just as the rock slide descended. When
the crashing noise stopped, he lay there all of a heap

with the rocks. They were little ones for the most part, but there was one big boulder, and it pinned down his leg.

Don ran towards Ed while the last of the rocks were still rolling. Ed had had the presence of mind to cover his head with his arms, and he lay with his head still covered. But he lay still.

"Ed, Ed!" Don cried.

A moment passed. Shorty, now unconcerned, grazed on some fresh moist grass. Tizz, more intelligent and sensitive, nuzzled at Don, as if she needed some re-assurance herself. Spot, who had been frightened, too, but without panicking, now set up a nervous barking.

It was the barking that reached into Ed's unconsciousness. He opened his eyes and looked up at Don's scared face. Being Ed, even in pain he tried to make a joke of it.

"Well," he said with an effort, "I guess I'll never win a medal for jumping, will I?"

"Ed, are you all right?"

He even managed to smile. "Who, me? I'm fine. I always like to rest like this, in a soft rock pile."

Ed tried to get up. Then he winced, and looked at the big boulder that lay against his leg. "Correction," he said, and Don noticed that his lips looked white. "I guess I'm not fine, after all. That boulder got me."

Don started clearing away the debris. The little rocks were easy to move, but the big one took some doing. It was easy to see from the way Ed lay, that the leg was broken.

"Ed," Don asked, trying to sound calm, "should I ride back and get Jerry?"

Ed was in pain, but he kept right on thinking. "No," he decided. "We're closer to Many Glacier now than to Going-to-the-Sun. And to Many Glacier it's a downhill trail, but you'd have an uphill climb back to Jerry." He winced again, then admitted, "I guess I'm going to need a doctor more than I'll need Jerry."

"I could ride Tizz to Many Glacier," Don suggested. He knew there was a big hotel there, and if there was a big hotel, there would most certainly be a ranger, and a doctor.

Ed asked, "Do you think you could make it alone?"

"Sure I could."

"Okay, try it."

Don turned to Tizz and Shorty. There was work to be done, and he hoped he knew how to do it. First he tethered Shorty carefully to a larch, using the kind of no-slip knot he had learned in Cub Scouts. Then he unfastened the cinch belt around Tizz's middle and removed the saddlebags. He had to let them fall to the ground because they were too heavy for him to handle alone, but he did not worry about that. He knew that the bags carried canned food for the most part.

"Tizz," he said to the pony, talking to her as Tracy always did, "you and I are going on a long ride."

He scrambled up on her back, and called to Ed, "I'm going. Will you be all right?"

"Sure," Ed assured him, managing another smile.

"You be careful, now. Remember to watch for sign-posts along the trail. Lots of luck."

Don felt a lump in his throat, but he answered, "Lots of luck to you, too."

He started off, and Tizz carefully stepped around the rubble of the avalanche to the clear path ahead. Then an unexpected problem came up. Spot ran right after Tizz, as he was in the habit of doing.

"Go back, Spot!" Don ordered.

Spot kept right on following.

Don tried again, and when his orders did not work, he knew there was only one thing to be done. He slid off Tizz's back and carried Spot to Ed. There he sat the dog down, and he gave him a firm slap as he commanded, "Stay!" He hated to do it, but he *had* to.

When he clambered up on Tizz's back and rode off, Don looked over his shoulder. Spot was following them only with his eyes this time, and his eyes were mournful, but he was staying. Don knew he would remain close to Ed, barking at any suspicious noise, sounding a warning that something was wrong to Jerry and the boys as they came along the trail.

He began his long ride, and this time he rode alone.

DON RIDES ALONE

The trail led downhill past a waterfall and along a swift-running creek, but Don did not notice the beautiful scenery. He was riding for badly needed help, and he was on his own. This was no time to get lost, so he kept his eyes open for trail markers.

Tizz did very well, too. There were many places where the going was tricky, slippery and rocky, but she picked her way through carefully, then went back to her rhythmic trot that could eat up distance.

When the trail entered a dense, dark forest, Don could feel a pulse beating in his throat. He pretended that the pulse was beating because he was getting tired and not because he was afraid.

There was a movement in some bushes, and he thought about bears, and how Ed had warned him never to go near a mother bear if she had a cub. He tried not to think what might happen if it were a bear with cubs in those bushes. When a big pheasant ran out, he felt greatly relieved. At another point, he saw what looked like the antlers of a moose, but when he

remembered how Harley had tricked him, he realized that these "antlers", too, were only some bare branches. Still, that ride in the forest seemed awfully long.

At last Don saw the trail marker he was looking for. It told him that Many Glacier Hotel was only a mile away. He took the fork in the trail that would bring him to it, and urged Tizz into a trot. Trotting bareback was not easy, but when he thought of Ed lying there in the trail, his own discomfort seemed like nothing.

As Don rode out of the forest, he could see the big, sprawling chalet-type Many Glacier Hotel down below. It was on a lake he knew was called Swiftcurrent, and the towering peaks across the water were reflected in it.

Even without the spectacular scenery, that hotel would have looked beautiful to him. He dug his knees into Tizz's sides and urged her on, for the last leg of his long ride. He had made it, and he had made it alone!

Help came out to meet him, as it happened. Riding down the foothill trail, Don met a group of college boys and girls, summer employees at the hotel, who were starting on a hike during their time off.

"What a cute pony!" one of the girls said.

Don felt at once that she was a friend. He asked "Can you tell me where I can find a doctor, or a ranger?"

Things happened quickly after that. The young people were not only eager to help, they gave up plans for their hike, and took over. In a few minutes, they had found the ranger.

He listened carefully to what Don had to tell him, then said: "It would be best to bring him in to the hotel and the doctor. I'll need four stretcher-bearers."

Four of the college boys volunteered at once. They all mounted horses and set out, the ranger in the lead. Although the horses were bigger, Tizz kept up very well and Don was proud of her. He noticed that when they went through the forest in a group, it was not nearly so dark as when he had gone through it alone.

As they approached the spot where Don had left Ed, he could hear voices, and he guessed that Jerry and the boys had arrived. He knew for a certainty that they had when another turn in the trail brought a welcome sight. Several of the boys were running to meet them, Harley among them. Don never thought that he would be glad to see Harley, but he was.

"Yea, you made it!" Harley yelled when he saw Don, and this time he wasn't making fun of him.

One switchback later, the party reached Ed. Jerry was at his side. He had given Ed first aid and aspirin, and had made a pillow out of a poncho.

Also, still at Ed's side, was Spot. He moved only when he saw that Don and Tizz had come back. Then he raced towards them, barking a joyous greeting, circling rapidly around Tizz the way he did when he was excited.

Ed hailed the party with a smile. "Don Hill to the rescue!" he called. "You made good time."

The ranger carefully tied some temporary splints to Ed's leg, and he was lifted to the stretcher. Then the long journey back began.

Jerry had helped repack Tizz, and he and Don went on ahead with the pony and Shorty. Don would rather have stayed behind with Ed, but taking care of Tizz was part of his job.

At the Many Glacier campsite, Don helped Jerry unpack Shorty and Tizz, as he would have helped Ed. Then he gave the horse and pony rub-downs, as Ed would have done. Meanwhile, Jerry and the boys set up camp and got supper ready.

For once, Don was not hungry. He kept thinking of Ed. The ranger had said Ed would be taken directly to the hotel where the doctor would be waiting. He wondered how long it would be before he could see his friend.

When Don could not stand it any longer, he called Spot and went over to Many Glacier Hotel. By this time it was dark, but there was a bright moon, and he could see his way quite well.

The ranger was in the lobby of the hotel. He recognized Don and greeted him with the good news that Ed was coming along fine. "The doctor said it was a clean break, no complications. But of course, he's not going to go on any more pack trips this summer."

Don's heart sank. He had really known this in the back of his mind since the accident, but he had not let the thought swim to the surface.

"Right now, Ed's sleeping," the ranger was going on, "but you'll be able to see him in the morning. In the meantime we ought to notify his parents. Do you know where he lives?"

"I don't have his home address," Don answered,

"but he worked for my uncle at the ranch, and I've got that telephone number right here." Don poked around in his pocket until he found the little notebook his uncle had given him with the telephone number in it, and handed it to the ranger.

The ranger accepted it with a smile. "How old are you, son?"

"Ten, sir," Don told him politely.

"You know, for a boy of ten, you've got a pretty good head on your shoulders."

The praise felt good to Don's ears. He said good-night to the ranger and turned to leave, feeling warm all over.

The warmth quickly chilled. As he turned, he saw Harley. What was worse, Harley got into step with him to walk back to the campsite.

"Did you follow me?" Don demanded hotly.

"Sure," Harley admitted readily. "I guessed this was where you were heading, and it gets pretty dark here at night. Besides, I wanted to know about Ed, too."

Spot, waiting outside, greeted Don with his usual show of affection. Then he ran alongside of him, snapping at moonbeams.

Harley seemed to be thinking something over. Then he said, "You know something? The ranger was right. You do have a pretty good head on your shoulders. I don't think I'd have been able to do what you did today, when I was only ten."

Don said nothing. How could he? He was speechless!

"And don't worry about Ed," Harley was going on. "My brother broke his leg last summer, and it healed all right, and he can do anything now."

Well, what do you know! Don thought in wonder. Harley wasn't such a bad guy, after all.

SURPRISE

The next morning when Don walked over to the hotel with Spot, there was Ed, sitting on the porch, his leg in a cast and propped up on a leather hassock. Several young people were with him.

"Here comes my rescuer," Ed called in a cheerful voice as he saw Don.

Face to face, Don didn't know exactly what to say. "Feel all right?" he asked, trying to sound casual.

"Sure, I feel fine," Ed replied. He looked fine, too. He tapped the leg cast, "All this amounts to now is that it's going to be a nuisance. But look at all the autographs I've got."

Don saw that the college girls and boys had written their names all over it. Ed invited Don to do the same, and he did.

"Say," Ed remembered as Don was writing, "this is the day the boys were to hike to Grinnell Glacier. They're getting a late start, aren't they?"

"No, they're gone. Jerry got them out early this morning."

Ed nodded. "Good. But how come you didn't go along?"

"I thought I'd better stick around here," Don told him. "I have to look after Tizz and Shorty."

"Tizz turned out to be a better horse than Shorty," Ed said with a wry smile. "Don't you ever let anyone tell you that pony isn't smart."

"I won't!"

Some of the young people suggested a game of bridge to help Ed pass the time. Don beat a hasty retreat. So far as he was concerned, bridge was for the birds, not for boys who were helpers on pack trips—even though right now that pack trip looked grounded.

Back at the campsite, Don fed and watered Tizz and Shorty. He gave both horses rub-downs and, while he had the time, he gave Tizz the kind of good grooming she was used to having when she was not being a pack pony. He rode her bareback as he had yesterday, to give her some exercise. Spot ran along for company.

Whenever they passed any people, Don would hear a murmur, "That's the boy who rode in alone from Piegan Pass on that pony, to get help for the one with the broken leg!" Don pretended not to hear the remarks, but he felt his chest swell with pride.

Still, the day was a long one. He didn't want to hang around the hotel and be a nuisance to Ed, who had plenty of company, so he did odds and ends around the camp, to help pass the time. At noon he found some food and fixed his own lunch, feeling kind of low. Ed would have to go home, he was thinking, and that meant the end of the line for him, too. He hated the thought of leaving this beautiful park, where there still was much that he had not seen. He had been looking forward to next week and Two Medicine Lake, and another meeting with Freddy Steppingstone, too.

So Don puttered around, thinking his own thoughts. He had just about decided that he might go back and see Ed by now without seeming too anxious, when one of the boys working at the hotel sought him out. "Where've you been hiding?" he asked. "Ed wants to see you. He's got a surprise."

"What's the surprise?" Don asked as, with Spot, he walked toward the big hotel.

The college boy chuckled. "If I told you, it wouldn't be a surprise, would it?"

That sounded reasonable enough to Don, so he

walked the rest of the way in silence.

He had to wait until he could walk around to the porch side to know what the surprise was. Then he knew right away. Because there, with Ed, were his Aunt Kate and his Uncle George. *And* Tracy.

Don was so glad to see his little sister that he ran right up to her and kissed her. Tracy was just as glad to see him.

So were his aunt and uncle. They had flown up, they told him, when they had heard about Ed. They were going to fly him back to the ranch and have him get well there.

"I won't be much good to you," Ed warned, "but maybe if I can't ride a horse, I can drive the jeep."

"Don't worry about that!" Uncle George said warmly. "If you don't do anything else, you can sit for Tracy. She'd love that. She's missed you badly."

"I've missed Don and Tizz, too," Tracy added quickly, blushing. She turned to Don. "Where's Tizz?"

"What are we waiting for?" Don replied. They raced out of the hotel, where Spot was waiting to be introduced. Then they ran to the campsite and Tizz.

It was a happy reunion. The pony was really glad to see her little mistress. She nudged and nuzzled her, and of course, Tracy had remembered to tuck a few carrots inside her jacket. Watching his sister, Don realized how much she had missed Tizz, and how unselfish she had been in letting him come on this trip with the pony.

"Tizz," Tracy said as she hugged her, "I heard all about you finding your way here with Don to get help, and I'm so proud of you!"

Tizz shook her head. Actually, she wanted to be free of those small arms of Tracy's which, while they were loving, were restraining. But it looked as if she were saying that she was pretty proud of herself, too.

From then on, the hours flew until the boys came back from their hike to the glacier. Don and Tracy were waiting to greet them, with Tizz and Spot. He introduced his sister to the group, and told Jerry that he was going to stay at the hotel for dinner.

During dinner, he and his family talked over plans. Uncle George said he figured the best thing to do would be to send Ed and Aunt Kate and Tracy home by plane, and then he would drive the pick-up truck with Tizz and Shorty in the trailer.

"You can come along with me, if you like, Don," his uncle said, "or you can fly back if you'd rather."

"I'd rather ride with you," Don decided. Having come out with Ed, he knew what a long trip it could be, alone. But he spoke without enthusiasm. Remembering how much fun it had been, driving to Glacier Park with Ed, he felt sad again at the thought that the adventure had ended so abruptly.

They were still at dinner when word came that someone was waiting to see them. The family went out to the porch, and there, of all people, was Harley! He looked all slicked up and had even put on a clean shirt.

He started to speak politely and seriously, and it sounded as if he had been rehearsing what he was going to say. "Sir," he said, and Uncle George, who was used to western informality, looked a little startled at being addressed so formally, "I was chosen to represent our outfit, and to tell you how sorry we all are about Ed's accident."

"Thanks," Uncle George answered, "but that couldn't be helped. Accidents do happen sometimes, though one like this might not happen again in a hundred years."

Harley nodded. "That's exactly how we feel, sir." He cleared his throat. "That's why we'd like to ask

you to let Don stay with us even if Ed must leave."

Uncle George showed his surprise. "Don, stay on alone?"

"Not alone, sir. With the rest of us boys, and Jerry, and another fellow who's on his way to take Ed's place."

Uncle George's forehead clouded. "Well, I don't know—"

As he paused, Harley went on: "The pack trip wouldn't be as much fun, without Don. He's younger than we are, but he's a real good sport. And Jerry said to tell you he's a lot of help, too."

Uncle George stopped looking undecided, and looked pleased, instead. "I'd say that's a pretty high compliment!" He turned to Don. "I think your father would say it was okay, if he were in my place. What do you say, Don?"

"I'd like to stay."

He didn't even have to think it over. The words welled right up by themselves, as if they were hiding just behind his tongue, waiting for the chance to be spoken. By the relief he felt as he spoke them, Don knew how much he had wanted to stay, and had hoped that he could.

Then, looking at Tracy, Don added, "That is, if Tracy wouldn't mind being without Tizz for a while longer."

Tracy had some deciding of her own to do. But she spoke up after only a moment, "No, I won't mind too much. I can keep on riding Frosty till you get back."

Aunt Kate added proudly, "And wait till you see how well Tracy can ride Frosty, too!"

"I'll bet!" Don said with enthusiasm. He turned to Ed, "Do you want to take Spot with you? He's your dog, too."

Ed shook his head. "Tizz needs Spot, for company. You bring him back when the trip is over."

"Then it's all settled?" Harley put in, dropping his polite and formal voice and sounding natural again. "Yea!"

He turned to Don. "The guys are waiting to hear what you'd say. Want to come back with me and tell them the good news?"

Don started for the campsite with Harley. The wind off the glaciers was cold.

"Let's run," Harley suggested.

Harley was bigger and could run faster, but he

hung back a little, so that he and Don could stay together.

Spot, running with them, barked at the moon. And Tizz, recognizing the bark of her friend, whinnied a greeting.